Starry Forest Books, Inc. • P.O. Box 1797, 217 East 70th Street, New York, NY 10021 • Starry Forest is a trademark of Starry Forest Books, Inc. • Text and Illustrations © 2017 by Starry Forest Books, Inc. • This 2017 edition published by Starry Forest Books, Inc. • All rights reserved. No part of this publication may be reproduced, stored in a retrieval system, or transmitted in any form or by any means (including electronic, mechanical, photocopying, recording, or otherwise) without prior written permission from the publisher. • ISBN 978-1-946260-11-6 • Manufactured in Huizhou City, Guangdong Province, China • Lot #: 2 4 6 8 10 9 7 5 3 1 • 07/17

Rumpelstiltskin

The Brothers Grimm

retold by Peter Clover

illustrated by Robert Dunn

In a faraway kingdom, there once lived an old miller who had a pretty, young daughter. One day, the miller was delivering flour to the palace kitchens when the king strolled by. The miller wanted the king to notice him, so he quickly made up a story and said, "I have a beautiful daughter who can spin straw into gold!"

The king raised a doubting eyebrow. "Really?" he asked in a royal voice. "Bring your daughter to the palace. Then we shall see!"

The next afternoon, when the miller arrived at the royal palace with his daughter, the king ordered the guards to take the miller straight to the dungeon.

The king led the miller's daughter away and locked her in a room filled with yellow straw. In the middle of the room sat a wooden spinning wheel.

"Spin this straw into gold by morning," said the king. "Or you will stay locked in this room, forever. And your father will never leave the dungeon."

The moment the king locked the door, the miller's daughter burst into tears. She had no idea how to spin straw into gold.

Suddenly, a crooked little man magically appeared.
"Why are you crying?" asked the little man.
"I have been ordered to spin this straw into gold by morning," sobbed the girl. "And I don't know how!"

"Hmmm…let me see," said the curious man as he twisted his
long red beard. "I can spin this straw into gold if you like," he said.

"You can?" cried the girl.

"Yes! But what will you give me in return?" asked the little man.

"I can give you my mother's necklace," said the girl. "Here, take it."

The crooked little man snatched the necklace from the miller's daughter and sat down at the spinning wheel. As the wheel turned slowly, it made a soft whirring sound. The girl soon fell asleep.

The next morning when she awoke, the sun was shining through
the window. The strange little man had gone. But…next to the spinning
wheel was a huge pile of golden thread!

When the king unlocked the door, he was amazed to find a pile of glittering gold where the straw had been. But the king was a greedy man. He immediately took the girl to a bigger room filled with even more straw.

"Spin this straw into gold," the king commanded, locking
the door behind him. "Or you will never see your father again."

At the sight of all that straw, the poor girl fell to her knees in tears.
She was sobbing so loud, she didn't hear the crooked little man
magically appear again.

"What will you give me if I spin this straw into gold?"
asked the little man.

The girl jumped with surprise. "Oh...it's you!"
she smiled. "All I have left is my mother's ring."

"I'll take it." he replied.

The curious little man grinned with glee as he slipped the ring onto his long, boney finger. Then he sat down at the spinning wheel. The wheel hummed, and the miller's daughter was soon fast asleep.

When she woke, it was morning. And once again, the room was filled with golden thread. Gold covered the bed, and gold covered the table. Gold was everywhere.

The king was overjoyed. But his eyes shone greedier than ever as he led the girl to the largest room in the palace. It was filled from floor to ceiling with yellow straw.

"If you spin this straw into gold," said the king, "I will free your father, and crown you as my queen."

Alone in the room, the girl once again hung her head in despair. She had never seen so much straw in her life. Suddenly, a voice made her jump.

"What will you give me if I spin this straw into gold?" asked the little man.

The girl looked up. "I have nothing left to give," she sobbed.

"Hmmm…let me see!" The goblin's
eyes twinkled. "I know," he said. "If I spin
the straw and you marry the king, will you
give me your firstborn child?"

The girl said "yes" straight away,
hoping that once she became queen
she would never see the little man again.

The next morning, the room was filled with a pyramid of glittering golden thread. The king was delighted. Immediately he set the miller free and made plans to marry the miller's daughter.

Later that year, the new queen had a beautiful baby boy. She had forgotten all about her promise to the crooked little man. So she was shocked when he suddenly appeared in the palace nursery.

"What do you want?" demanded the queen.

"The baby," he hissed. "I have come to take what you promised me."

The queen hugged her baby close. "I am rich. I will give you all the gold you can carry," she said. "But please don't take my baby."

"NO!" said the goblin, angrily.

"I want what you promised me. Your firstborn child, remember?"

The queen wanted to scream, but her voice was frozen with fear.

The little man had an idea.

"Hmmm…let me see!" he said. "I will give you three days. If you can guess my name by the end of the third day, you can keep your precious little prince." The queen agreed, and the goblin disappeared. The echo of his laughter filled the nursery.

The queen stayed awake all night, making a list of
all the names she could think of. The list grew and grew.

But when the little man came back the next day, he shook his head.
His name was not among them.

On the second day, the queen sent out a servant to collect the most unusual names in the kingdom. When the crooked little man came again, the queen asked, "Is it Spindleshanks? Hunkleberry? Spiderwick?" Her list was even longer than before. But the goblin shook his head and laughed.

The queen was desperate. She couldn't face the third day. As twilight fell,
she went to the forest, hoping to find a secret place to hide her child.
Unexpectedly, the queen discovered a tiny cottage. A fire burned outside,
and the strange little man was dancing around the flames, singing.

From her hiding place the queen watched the crooked little man dancing and singing. She listened carefully to his song:

"They are big and I am small,
Yet I am smarter than them all.
She made a deal, she crossed the line,
Her little prince will soon be mine.
And she will never win this game,
For Rumpelstiltskin is my name."

"Rumpelstiltskin!" she whispered. A huge smile spread across her face as she hurried back to the palace with her secret.

The queen waited in the nursery for the morning sun to rise. Finally, the wicked goblin appeared. "Well, my queen," asked the little man. "This is your last chance! What is my name?"

"Hmmm … let me see!" said the queen. "It's not Harry or Henry is it? And it's not John or Jemmy?"

The goblin jumped up and down, shaking his head.

"And it's not Caspar, Melchior, or Balthazar?"

"No! No! No!" said the goblin with glee.

"Then it must be … Rumpelstiltskin," smiled the queen triumphantly.

"Noooooooooooooooo!!!" screamed Rumpelstiltskin. "You must have cheated! Cheat! Cheat!" The angry little man stomped his feet and tore at his beard and hair.

He was so furious that he burst into golden flames.

And he was never, EVER seen again.